USA TODAY BESTSI

SKYE MAC

Thud

CATNIP ASSASSINS
CHRISTMAS SPECIAL

Thud © 2021 by Skye MacKinnon

All rights reserved.

No part of this book may be reproduced in any form or by any electronic or mechanical means, including information storage and retrieval systems, without written permission from the author, except for the use of brief quotations in a book review.

Cover by Ravenborn Covers.

Published by Peryton Press.

skyemackinnon.com

Contents

For Anika/Ravenborn.
Thank you for the purrfect covers!

Author's Note

This book is best enjoyed with a blanket, some candles, a lit Christmas tree, a purring cat and a glass of mulled wine. I can't help with the first four, but there's a recipe for mulled wine at the end.

If you are deeply religious, you might find some parts of this story offensive. Forgive me. Kat made me write it.

You don't need to have read the other Catnip Assassins books to enjoy Thud, but if you want to, start with Meow (also available as audiobook).

And finally, subscribe to my newsletter for updates about new releases: skyemackinnon.com/newsletter.

You'll even get a free book for subscribing, so it's totally worth it.

Chapter One

I'm going to kill whoever came up with the idea that holidays are supposed to be relaxing.

They're not.

I'm dying of boredom.

Take a week off, they said. It will be fun, they said. Just read and go for walks and enjoy the peacefulness, they said. Sleep in, have breakfast in bed, they said.

Bah. The only way I'm going to survive the next five days is in a catnip-induced coma.

Have you ever had breakfast in bed? It's uncomfortable and two days later, I still find breadcrumbs on my sheets. Not that I'm obsessed with cleanliness, but I prefer not to wake up because something is itching me between my boobs – like last night. Besides, the echo of the smell of food is making me peckish at night.

The guys aren't faring much better. We've become so used to a house full of noise and kitten-induced chaos that silence feels almost threatening.

Lennox takes a sip of his eggnog and sighs. "Is it over yet?"

"Five more days," Ryker groans. "Is it possible that time stopped flowing? It feels like this day has lasted longer than it should."

"And it's only lunchtime," Gryphon adds, lounging on the sofa with an open book on his chest. "All this time, I thought I wanted a break, but now I realise how wrong I was."

"Maybe we should call them and ask to come back," Ryker suggests.

I shake my head. "No, that would be giving in. I don't think Aunt Rose would let the children leave, anyway. She's been looking forward to this for months."

"Yeah, she's missed having the twins there to boss around," Gryphon chuckles. "Her nest has only been empty for half a year, yet she behaves like she's been on her own for a decade."

My sisters Four and Ivy left Aunt Rose to go to university. I can't believe they're actually doing it, but once they had the idea, there was no stopping them. From what they've told me in their rare phone calls, they're the only shifters on campus, with the exception of one teacher who's turned out to be a werewolf. Four chose to do forensic studies, but Ivy surprised us all when she announced she'd become a teacher. I cannot imagine her in a classroom, no way, but she's decided that she's doing it and so it will happen.

With her house empty, Aunt Rose had been begging us to let the children visit her, luring us with promises of how nice it would be without them. She even bribed Caitlin and Pumpkin to come along, making sure that the guys and I would be truly on our own. Aunt Rose is pure evil.

I sigh. "Lennox, I think it's time you tell me where the catnip is hidden."

Gryphon laughs. "Yes, tell her, it will be entertaining for all of us. Remember last time? The way she rubbed against the postman? The poor guy almost peed himself."

I shoot daggers at him. I'd throw one if I wasn't wearing just a woolly jumper and tights. Being a mother to four inquisitive children has taught me not to wear blades in the house. They're all locked away safely, although the kids still manage to find the occasional weapon from time to time. No idea how they do it. They seem to have a sensor that attracts them to dangerous items. Only last week we found Bella serving her dolls deadly poison. And yes, she knew that's what it was. I make a mental note to speak to Bethany about that. I'm sure she's the source of the poison, especially since she's been begging me to let her teach the children how to spot poison in their food. I told her no, but only because I'd already done that. We've not had any attacks on our family since we eradicated Attenburgh's siren population four years ago, but you never know. I want them to be prepared.

"No catnip," Lennox says sternly. "How about we play a game?"

"How best to torture a wolf?" I suggest with a sly grin. I wish he hadn't found a way to hermetically seal the catnip supplies, preventing me from sniffing them out. He keeps changing the location, too, and after I found his stores the last time, he says he's put a number lock on it. That man is pure evil.

The phone rings and I'm on my feet in an instant, grateful for the distraction.

"Hello?"

"Kat!" Lily's voice comes through the crackling speaker. Our house is in the middle of nowhere, which shows in both our phone and television signals being unreliable. "Just the kitty I wanted to talk to."

"What's up?" I ask, ignoring her calling me *kitty*.

"I hate to disrupt your holiday..."

"Disrupt away!"

"Thought so," she snickers. "I can't imagine you sitting still, relaxing. How are the guys doing?"

"Similarly. What's the disruption? Please tell me it's an assassination? A bloody one?"

"Almost. We've been asked to investigate a murder case and, well, we're having trouble figuring out what happened. I thought you might be able to give us a second opinion."

As much as I would have preferred a good old killing, this is still miles better than sitting in our living room, twiddling my thumbs.

"What's the issue?"

"The murder weapon...well, it was a tree. And it's not making sense. I'm just about to head out there again, do you have time to meet me at the crime scene?"

"A tree?"

"It'll be easier to show you. Will you come?"

I smile and roll my shoulders. "On the way."

The guys refused to let me come on my own, so now all four of us wait at the edge of the Kidminster Woods to the west of Attenburgh. It's a cold but beautiful day and I greedily breathe in the fresh air. It smells like snow, but likely not until tomorrow.

I've been in this forest before, but not often enough to really know my way around. I usually go for runs closer to home. Especially when my litter of naughtiness decides to join me. They're full of energy, but their paws are a lot smaller than mine. Exhausting them is a great strategy, but having to carry them home on my back is too much work.

Lily meets us in a small clearing next to a ruined log cabin. I sniff the air. I can just about make out a trace of old blood. Very old. Someone died in that cabin but it was years ago. Not the murder we're here about.

"Finally, I was beginning to grow roots," she greets us. "Get it? Because of the trees. Roots."

I roll my eyes at her. "You've not become any better at jokes since you took over M.E.O.W. I thought my clever wit would have passed on to you by now."

"Clever wit. Sure. As if." She grins. "It's good to see you again. Did you think about what we discussed a month ago?"

"Yes. And no. I need more time to decide."

She'd asked me if I want to return to work. To be fair, I've been doing odd jobs for M.E.O.W. ever since the kittens were weaned, but it's been quite refreshing not to be in charge. When Lily told me that she's got plans to have a litter of her own, I thought she was joking. But if she really goes through with that plan, we're going to have to restructure M.E.O.W. Benjamin isn't ready to take the helm. Neither are the two new assassins Lily employed. And Bethany spends more time with us than at the headquarters. No, I'd be the only one who could be in charge. But I'm not sure I want to. That was my old life. I have a new one now. I've changed. I'm no longer the Kat I used to be. Haunted by her past, pursued by her enemies, a loner always scared to get close to others.

Nope, definitely not me anymore.

"Where's the tree?" Ryker asks, distracting me from my thoughts.

Right. We're here about a murder. Focus, Kat. This is going to be fun.

"Follow me," Lilly says and leads us further into the woods. We keep to an animal track that skirts around the undergrowth to avoid having our legs scratched by thorns and sharp little branches.

I let my senses expand, relishing in the silence around us. We're the only humans - well, demi-humans - for miles. High above in the trees, birds are watching us. I sense a squirrel to my right and resist the urge to chase it. Any larger animals that were here before we arrived have fled to a safe distance. I can just about smell a few deer to the North, but they're at least half a mile to the North.

Then, the scent of blood hits my nose. I grin and breathe in deep. I shouldn't be this excited. Someone died. I should feel sorry for them. Instead, I fasten my steps, almost bumping into Lily.

She turns around and gives me a knowing look. "Admit it, you missed this."

I step around her to take in the scene. On the phone she'd said that a man had been killed by a tree. I'd imagined him being crushed or maybe stabbed by a branch. I'd not expected the tree to be *inside* the man.

He's lying on his side, his bloodshot eyes staring into nothingness. His mouth is wide open, his jaws pushed open by the crown of the fir tree. It looks as if he tried to swallow it. The tree isn't big, only three metres tall, but quite a large part of it is inside the man.

"What the heck?" Lennox mutters as he joins me. "Did he try to deepthroat the tree?"

"Not appropriate," Lily says but her lips quiver with a suppressed smile. "See the trunk? Someone chopped it off, it wasn't torn from the ground, but we didn't find an axe."

I nod. "That means the murderer took it. Even if the victim cut the tree and then voluntarily impaled himself on it, someone took the axe."

"Why would anyone do this voluntarily?" Gryphon asks. He slowly walks around the crime scene, his eyes glowing with excitement. He's missed this as much as I have.

"I said 'if'. I doubt he did it to himself. Most humans have enough self-preservation instinct not to swallow a tree whole. He wouldn't have been able to push it in this far, not in that position. Someone very strong did this."

I try to lift the tree trunk, but it's too heavy. If I engaged my shifter strength, I could move it, but it's unlikely that I could stuff it down a struggling victim's throat. And this one clearly fought his attacker. His arms are covered in bruises and scratches. Most of his face is hidden by fir needles, but I'm pretty sure I can spot some bruising that isn't just from the impact of the tree hitting his mouth.

"This must be the weirdest murder weapon ever," Ryker says. He takes a deep breath. "I can't sense any shifters. You, Kat? Lennox?"

I shake my head. "No, only humans have been here. This isn't a supernatural murder. It's plain old human."

"That changes things," Lily says. "I assumed someone non-human was responsible, but I needed you guys to confirm it. If this really was done by a human, I need to change my strategy."

"Two humans, at least," Lennox points out. He's sniffing the dead guy's shirt. If he wasn't a shifter, this would be really weird.

"One male, one female. She's in heat."

"That's not what it's called," Lily chastises him. "Don't talk about women like we're Kats."

"Hey, it's not my fault that I sometimes went into heat," I snapped. "Besides, it's not happened again since giving birth. The ultimate cure to heat problems and acne."

Lily grins "I could do with a cure against acne."

"You've never had a single pimple. You're half succubus. I highly doubt succubi ever get them."

"Not for me," she says mysteriously. "But anyway. You do your sniffing thing, then meet me back at

M.E.O.W. in town. I have to head off, clients to see, money to earn, poisons to brew."

She gives us a cheerful wave before disappearing into the undergrowth. I look into empty space for a few seconds while getting my head around the fact that my former employee just told me what to do.

No, this doesn't feel right at all.

Chapter Two

I've avoided going to the M.E.O.W. headquarters ever since I handed on the baton. It gives me a severe case of jealousy and reminiscence paired with an unhealthy dose of adrenaline. It's not good of me to be here. It makes me want to go back to my old life, at least in part, and that's not what my kittens need from me. They need their mother, someone who occasionally shows emotions and who loves them from the intact part of her bruised heart. They don't need who I used to be. I'm not sure I'd like that Kat of the past if I met her on the streets now. She was egotistical, arrogant and convinced she had to push everyone away.

"We're upstairs!" Benjamin shouts at the top of his lungs. Just like old times. He never quite understood just how well us shifters can hear.

Behind me, Ryker chuckles.

We make our way to the upper floor which houses Lily's office and a meeting room. Downstairs is the posh consultation room where they meet clients. Lots of leather, polished wood and weapons on the walls to make an intimidating first impression. Up here, it's a different affair. The room contains four completely different looking sofas that they probably found on a skip. Crumbs and other food traces litter the carpet. The only similarity is that yet again, weapons are everywhere. I've got my eyes on a tiny dagger haphazardly balancing on the top of the window frame. A gemstone is embedded in the hilt. Pretty.

While my mates take their seats, I'm pulled towards that dagger. With a quick look to make sure nobody's watching, I reach up and pocket it as fast as I can. Only once it's safely in one of the leather-lined pockets of my trousers do I join the guys. The sofa smells like crisps and stale beer. Does Lily throw parties up here? Or is that her employees?

Lily finally deigns to leave her office. She hands out thin case files before hurrying away again to make tea. I study the folder, ignoring the page about the crime scene's location and historic information about the forest. I don't think that's relevant, but Lily probably included it to make the file look bigger. What interests me more is the quick summary about the victim.

Name: Geoffrey Baker

Age: 46

Relationship status: divorced

Profession: Cook

A cook. Not exactly a job that gets you killed. Unless you give a crime boss an overly salted meal, I suppose.

"Who did he work for?" I shout.

"Give me a second!" Lily sounds annoyed. Hey, I never asked her to make us tea. She could be sitting here with us. Instead, she's treating us like guests or clients rather than family. We should have met at our house instead.

"I'll have the cats scout out his home," Ryker says, his eyes fixed to the page. "Maybe they'll pick up any strange scents."

"Good idea. If we can't get more information from his place of work, we can go to his home and take a look ourselves."

Lily finally returns with a tray stacked with mugs and a chipped tea pot. Since when do I care whether crockery is chipped? I groan internally. I'm turning into a housewife. Worst. Nightmare. Ever.

"Let me do that," Gryphon offers helpfully. Always the good samaritan. "You tell us what we need to know."

Lily looks like she's about to argue, then shrugs and takes a seat. "Alright. He's a full-time employee at an organisation calling themselves the Womb of the Tree. Yes, you heard that correctly. The others are still collecting info on them, but it looks like they're some sort of cult. On the outside, they portray themselves as a retreat and self-improvement centre, but everything I've seen so far screams cult to me."

"What do they worship?" I ask. "Are they basically tree huggers?"

"It's surprisingly hard to find out. I've got one of their brochures, but it only talks about going back to nature and how spending time in the forest can help you relax. How it can help in putting one's life back together. It doesn't go into more detail. I think we'll have to do our own research." She grins widely. "How do you feel about infiltrating a tree cult?"

I exchange a look with the guys. That sounds a lot better than lounging at home with nothing to do. I'm sure we'll be done by the time the kids return.

My mates all nod their approval. Lennox looks as if he's ready to jump up right away. I know the feeling. This adventure can't start soon enough.

By the time we arrive at the Womb of the Tree's estate, I've come up with a false identity for myself. I'm Kate, widow and orphan, accompanied by her three adoptive brothers. It might be a bit over the top, but cults crave vulnerable people to prey on, right?

I've changed into clothes Lily provided. Rags and frayed cotton instead of expensive leather. She even smeared some dirt into my hair and on my cheeks. The guys got a similar treatment. We could have improved out disguises a little more, but we've been laying low for years so it's not as important as it would have been back when we were still actively working as assassins. Maybe this prolonged maternity leave had its good sides. With the death of the sirens, our enemies vanished overnight. We've been able to relax. Question is, have we lost our touch or are we all still the killers we used to be?

Time to find out.

I knock on the green double doors. Tree branches are carved into the wood, but they look more menacing than pretty. The Womb of the Tree occupy an entire block of buildings at the edge of town, fenced off by high brick walls. It's a miracle I hadn't heard of them before. But then, I've been busy changing nappies and singing lullabies.

25

With an ominous screak, the door opens, revealing a heavy set man in ruby red robes. A shaggy, unkempt beard looks like it could house several generations of fleas. He takes us in, then a smile appears on his withered face.

"How can I help you?"

"I'm Kate," I say in a pathetically weak voice. "These are my brothers. We heard this is a place of refuge. We have nowhere else to go."

His gaze wonders over our little group. I hope the guys are making themselves look innocent and non-threatening. It'll be hard for them, muscle-packed as they are, but hopefully the rags disguise most of their prowess.

"You are right, we are a refuge. How did you hear about us?"

"There was a woman in the street," I lie. Lily said the Womb cultists like to hang out around street corners, handing out leaflets and preaching their message. "She told me about this place. I lost my home when my husband passed away and..." I make my voice trail off while rubbing my dry eyes. I'd love to be able to cry on command but that's not one of my many skills.

"I'm so sorry to hear that," the man says. He's still smiling but he looks at us like a predator drools over prey. He's taken the bait. "And these are your brothers?"

I smile shily. "Adoptive. We grew up together in an orphanage and they stayed with me when I married my husband to help out on the farm. We're very close."

Behind me, Lennox chortles. I want to kick him, but luckily, it was quiet enough for the man not to hear.

The cultist turns his attention to my men, his interest piqued. "You worked on a farm?"

"We did," Gryphon confirms. His voice sounds rougher than usual. Nice acting indeed. "But our beloved sister's husband was deep in debt, so when he passed, she had to sell the farm. We all lost our home from one day to the next."

For a moment, the man stays quiet and I worry that he's not swallowed the bait, but then his smile widens. "You have come to the right place. We are always willing to welcome new members to our family. We can provide you with a home and work. We have our own fields where we grow most of the food for the community."

Lily was right in suggesting that the guys pose as farmers. I won't tell her, of course, or she'll become too buoyant for her own good.

We follow the guy inside the compound. A large fir tree stands in the centre of a courtyard. The image of the dead guy deepthroating the same kind of tree pops into my head and I have to force myself to keep my expression blank. I don't think I'll ever be able to look at evergreen trees the same way again.

Our guide bows deep to the tree and whispers a prayer under his breath. Something like 'oh holy tree', but his words were too slurred to understand.

"This is the Father," he says when the turns around to us. "The lord of all trees. We will see the Mother and her Womb in a moment when I take you to our guest quarters. For now, you'll be able to stay there until we find you more permanent accommodation in the acolyte wing."

He's deranged. Lord of trees? This guy has smoked a few too many pine needles.

"Do you want us to bow?" Ryker asks to my surprise.

The cultist seems taken aback. "We don't expect you to. For now, you'll be laymen – and laywomen, miss – until you learn more about our teachings and beliefs. Only when you become acolytes, you're required to follow our customs."

When, not if. He doesn't have any doubts that we'll subscribe to their religion. That will make our job easier.

"But come now, follow me. We're going to have dinner soon, which will give you the chance to meet more of your new family."

He leads us through a series of smaller buildings until we enter another courtyard, exactly the same size as the first. The tree in the centre is much larger and its trunk has a strange gnarly outgrowth at the front. That must be the Mother. The Womb growth is almost as tall as me and several times as wide. A tumour, maybe?

Two women are doing something to the Womb, pushing metal spikes into it. One of them attaches a rubber tube to the spike.

"Are they collecting the tree's sap?" Gryphon asks before I can.

The cultist nods. "They are harvesting the Mother's Gift. It's our most holy sacrament. You will be taught all about it soon."

He bows to the tree, deeper than to the Father, and whispers yet more prayers. I'm not sure yet if he's pretending or if he actually worships the trees.

"You are joining us just at the right time," he says as he leads us along the side of the courtyard. "In two days, we're celebrating the Birth. It is our biggest ceremony of the year, so everyone's very excited. But more about that later. Here we are, our guest quarters."

He unlocks a door and bids us to step inside. Eight doors lead off a narrow corridor.

"Rooms two and four are free," the man says after checking a blackboard near the entrance. "Miss Kate, you can have room two and your brothers can share room four. Bathrooms are at the end of the hallway. I will get one of the acolytes to bring you towels and fresh clothes."

I give him my best smile. "Thank you so much. We really appreciate it."

"You are very welcome. I'll give you a moment to get settled, then I shall show you the dining hall. Just in time for dinner, as it happens. It's always good to get there first." He grins and pats his large belly. "You don't want to miss out on all the delicacies our cook-"

His smile disappears and he looks disappointed. "I forgot. Our cook is currently...absent. I guess it'll be sandwiches again."

"We're grateful for any food you'll share with us," I say quickly. "Is your cook on holiday?"

"Something like that." Most people wouldn't have been able to detect that as a lie. I see the tells and I know my mates will have, too, but it's good to know that we're dealing with a very experienced liar.

He turns to leave. "I will see you later."

"Wait. I never caught your name."

He pushes back his shoulders. "My name is Nikolaus and I'm the leader of this family."

Chapter Three

I have no intentions of sleeping in my room, but I pull back the duvet and put my little bag on the bed to make it look as if I will. The guys are in a large room with two double and two single beds, so we'll arrange those to suit us. Not that we'll get much sleep. I have full intentions to scope out the compound tonight and search for any clues to the cook's murder.

A young woman, barely out of her teens, knocks on my door, carrying a stack of towels. She introduces herself as Mary, a name as innocent as she looks.

"Brother Nikolaus asked me to bring you these," she mutters without making eye contact. "And I am to show you to the dining hall."

When I take the towels, I realise that they were hiding a baby bump. She's quite far along in her pregnancy, maybe seven or eight months. I don't know enough about human pregnancies to be certain, but she's definitely almost ready to pop.

I whistle for the guys and a moment later, they spill from their room. The girl's eyes widen at the sight of my three men. She looks as if she's about to run away. She reminds me of a skittish deer.

She hurries off, her gait wobbly with the extra weight, and I assume we're supposed to follow. I catch up with her when we step back into the courtyard.

"Have you lived here long?" I ask.

"All my life."

I had no idea the cult has existed for that long. Fascinating. At least they're all still alive, so it's probably not a suicide cult. They might be harmless...but if that was the case, then Nikolaus wouldn't have had to lie about the cook's death. No, the murder is connected to the cult and I'm going to find out how.

Mary bows to the Mother as deeply as she can with the bump in the way while muttering prayers. This time, I can make out all the words. 'Oh Mother tree, Oh Mother tree, your gifts are here for all to see. Oh Mother tree, Oh Mother tree, I love the Father and worship thee.'

Weirdest prayer ever. I wonder if everyone in this cult is crazy. I guess you have to be to deify trees.

We walk through an open-arced cloister until we get to a building in the centre of the compound. Other red-robed cultists join us as we enter the dining hall. It's surprisingly quiet inside. It seems everyone eats in silence. The sound of cutlery hitting plates echoes through the large room. We get some curious looks, but nobody meets our eyes.

While we queue up for food, I examine the crowd. Everyone wears the same blood-red robes, but some cultists have elaborately stitched hems around the neckline and their sleeves. That must be a sign of being higher up in the hierarchy. The men all have beards while the women wear their long hair braided. There are only a few children, ranging from toddler to adolescent, but they wear the same red robes as the adults. If my kittens were here, they'd be chatting, shouting, misbehaving. These children are the exact opposite. They don't have the same spark.

A woman hands me a plate and I grab two sandwiches without taking note of the fillings. Behind me, Lennox audibly sniffs the air before making his choice. He's always been more fussy when it comes to food. Back at the Pack, we ate whatever we got, little as it was, but once he escaped, he became pickier.

Mary has disappeared into the crowd, so I choose a random table that has two other women sitting there already. The older one looks a vaguely familiar, but I can't remember where I might have seen her before. I probably haven't. I'd remember the red robes.

They both smile at us before putting their attention back on their food. I'd hoped to gather information during dinner, but instead we eat in silence. The bread is delicious, definitely homemade, but the cheese is tasteless and dry.

Nobody gets up after they've finished, so we do the same and wait. I scan the hall, looking for anything that stands out. But every single one of the about fifty cultists acts in the same boring, uninspired way. They all stare at their empty plates without making eye contact or whispering. They sit in groups, separated by gender, but it feels like everyone's by themselves. How sad. And that says a lot coming from me, a former lone panther.

When all plates are cleared, Nikolaus gets up and clears his throat.

"Brothers and Sisters, please join me in welcoming our newest arrivals, Kate and her brothers. They've been through a lot, so we will do our best to make them feel at home. Would anyone like to volunteer to be their mentors during their first week?"

One young man with an impressive ginger beard raises his hand at the same time as the older woman at our table gets up.

"Wonderful. Joe, you will be responsible for the men while you, Angie, will look after Kate."

The woman, Angie, gives me a warm smile as she takes her seat again. It's the first genuine emotion I've seen displayed since arriving at the compound.

"Tomorrow, at the Eve of the Birth, we will gather here to celebrate, but until then, you all know that a lot of work still needs to be done. You all have your tasks and I'm confident you will complete them in time for the celebrations. Elders, please join me in my study. Everyone else, sleep well."

That's the signal dinner is over. The cultists get up and stream out of the hall, still completely silent. The ginger man who volunteered to take care of the guys comes over to our table and motions us to follow him. When I move to follow him, Angie grabs my wrist and shakes her head. She pulls me in the opposite direction, away from the guys. I wave them goodbye. Gryphon shoots me an amused smile, as if he's having fun. Weirdo.

As soon as we step outside, noise hit me. People are finally talking to each other. It's reassuring to know that this rule of silence only applies during dinner. It'll make it a lot easier to gather intelligence if we can talk to the cultists.

Angie leads me to a bench under one of the cloister arches. The sun set while we were inside and it's freezing, but the older woman doesn't seem to care.

I draw on some of my shifter energy to increase my body temperature. I don't like feeling cold.

"I'm glad you chose to join us," Angie says and gives me another warm smile. "We've not had any new arrivals in a while."

"It sounded like a good place to go," I reply, returning her smile.

"That it is. And you arrived just at the right time. Tomorrow is the Eve and the day after we celebrate the Birth. Our Mother has been looking forward to it. It seems she's carrying twins and can't wait to finally give birth."

Wait, what?

"Are we talking about the tree?" I ask.

Angie chuckles. "In a way. How much do you know about the Womb of the Tree?"

"Almost nothing. Just what it said on the leaflet that we were given."

"Ah, that's how you found out about us?"

I nod.

"Then I shall start at the beginning. We worship the Mother and the Father, represented by the trees in the courtyards. The Creators started off as a single tree, so large that its branches embraced the entire world. Through their love, they multiplied, creating all of nature, from the smallest seed to the tallest tree.

"But over time, the Mother and the Father grew too big. Sunlight no longer reached the earth and their creation suffered. To save their children, they sacrificed themselves. They caused an almighty storm and through the power of a thousand lightning strikes, they burst into flame. Ash rained down on the earth, creating new life wherever it fell. That's when the first humans were born. We all carry part of the Creators with in it. We were born from their ashes, created through their sacrifice."

She pauses for dramatic effect, giving me the chance to process her words. We're basically all part tree. Got it.

"To honour their endless love, we celebrate the Birth every year. A representative of the Father and a servant of the Mother will join eight months before the celebration, creating the seed that will be carried until it is time. During these eight months, they are known as the Mother and the Father themselves. It is the responsibility of all of us to ensure their wellbeing and comfort."

"Wait, let me get this straight. You're saying a man and a woman from this community had sex eight months ago and the woman will give birth the day after tomorrow?"

"Crudely put, but correct."

"Why eight months, not nine?"

"Before we had the knowledge to induce a birth, we conducted the inception nine months before the celebration, but that meant we had to hope that the Mother would give birth on the correct day. Now, we make sure she does."

"And what happens to the child?"

She gives me a strange look. "What do you expect? They're raised by the community as our most valued members of the family. They're pure, like those of us who joined as adults can never be. They were touched by the Creators, blessed by them."

Phew. For once, I've found a cult that doesn't delight in hurting children. Such a nice change from what I've dealt with in the past.

I remember the pregnant girl who brought us our towels and put two and two together. "Mary is this year's Mother? And she said she's lived here since birth, so was she one of the children?"

Angie's expression darkens. "Mary is not the Mother. It's getting late. You should sleep. We start the day early and tomorrow will be even earlier than usual. There's still so much to prepare for the celebrations. What are your skills? Can you cook? Sew?"

I'm pretty good at sewing wounds, but I don't tell her that. And I can make poisons and potions, but I'm generally told to stay out of the kitchen.

"No. Sorry."

"Then you'll clean," she decides. "I'll find out where you're most needed and I'll take you there tomorrow morning."

She leads me back to the guest rooms without another word. I hit a nerve when I mentioned Mary. Not the Mother, that means she got pregnant outside of their weird ritual. Is that allowed? Angie's reaction makes me think not. That could be a motive for murder. Maybe Geoffrey Baker was the baby's father. Maybe that's why he was killed.

But it's too early to jump to conclusions.

I wait in my room until the guys return. Someone left a white robe on my bed along with a simple linen nightgown. After taking a look at the bathroom, I decide not to take a shower. I'm not a clean freak but I'm pretty sure there are things living in the mould on the walls.

Even though Nikolaus made it sound as if only two rooms in the guest wing were empty, I don't sense any other people in this part of the building. Well, as soon as everyone's gone to bed, I shall start here, exploring the other guest rooms.

By the time my mates arrive, I'm bored out of my mind. I didn't bring any books or other entertainment, so all I can do is stare at the bland walls and start theories about who killed Geoffrey Baker and why.

"Honey, we're home!" Lennox calls before they burst into my room. They left their guide at the front door, so we're alone.

Ryker lifts me into his strong arms and carries me over into their room. Usually, I'd complain, but I'm tired and glad to have them near me again. They all pile on the beds, looking at me expectantly.

Lennox takes my hand, rubbing my fingernails the way he loves to. Weirdo. "What did you find out? And before you ask, all we got was a tour of the estate and a lecture about how they work their fields. Absolutely nothing about their beliefs. Joe blocked all questions in that direction."

"Wow, I guess I had more luck then." I fill them in on what I learned from Angie.

"They breed baby trees." Gryphon looks somewhere between humour and disgust. "That's so weird."

"You can say that again. I wonder who the Mother and the Father are. Mary's the only pregnant woman I've seen and Angie said it wasn't her."

"It's not going to be easy to find out by sneaking around," Lennox says with a yawn. "It'll be better to try and talk to the cultists tomorrow. Sounds like we'll be on the fields all day, so that should give us plenty of opportunities to chat with some of the men. What are they making you do?"

"Clean," I groan. "Can't say I'm looking forward to it."

Gryphon grins widely. "It'll be good for you. Might teach you a thing or two."

I hiss at him. "I've told you, I'm not a housecat. I don't do housework. Or at least not more than my share."

At home, we each have our chores, including the children and our many stray cats. We're too many people – and felines – for just one person to look after the household. My sisters know that whenever they stay at our house, they're expected to pitch in.

I climb off the bed and stretch. "Shall we take a look around?"

Chapter Four

Out of the eight rooms in the guest quarters, four are covered in dust at least an inch deep. No one has set foot in those in months if not years. One room looks like it's been used recently, with a rumpled up duvet still on the bed. I sniff at the fabric. The scent isn't familiar but I commit it to memory just in case.

The final room is the most interesting.

"Blood," Lennox says as soon as we enter.

I nod. I can smell it too, despite the stench of vinegar and bleach. Someone's tried to erase all traces of whatever happened in here, but they weren't thorough enough.

I spot a tiny row of blood droplets on the door frame. The blood has seeped into the wood, making it impossible to remove. They're not enough to smell whose blood it is, but the familiar scent clinging to the bed solves that mystery. Geoffrey Baker. The scent is heavy enough to make it clear that he slept in here, lived in here. I thought he was part of the cult, so why would he sleep in the guest quarters?

"Look at the lock," Gryphon points out. "The door was locked regularly. And see the scratches on the door? He was locked in here and couldn't get out."

"It's the only room without a window," Ryker muses. "They used it as a cell. A prison."

I wet my finger and rub it over the blood splatters, then lick it. "Two days at most. He was attacked in here shortly before he got killed in the forest. He was definitely murdered there and he was conscious while they pushed the tree down his throat, but why? It would have been much easier to simply kill him here. Strangle him, stab him, poison him. So many options. Why go through all the trouble?"

"Because we're dealing with a cult," Gryphon says. "And they believe that trees are more than just trees. Being killed by one would be a sentence carried out not by humans, but by their deities."

"That makes sense. Maybe this wasn't a murder done in secret. Maybe it was an execution."

My mind goes into a flurry of possibilities. There were at least two humans at the crime scene, one man and one woman.

"Lennox, you said you smelled a female in heat back in the forest. Could she have been pregnant or was she just ovulating?"

He shrugs. "It was too faint to know for sure. Lots of hormones, though, so I suppose it could have been a pregnant female. I've not been around enough breeding humans to be certain of the difference. And you smelled very different when you were pregnant."

"Is that a compliment?"

"If you want it to be."

"Smooth," Gryphon snickers. "What now?"

"Now, we're going to find the Mother and the Father. Lennox, since you clearly excel at sniffing out females, you're with me. Ryker and Gryphon, you see if you can't find out who the Father is. Let's not stay out too late, though. It sounds like they're going to make us work hard tomorrow."

Climbing over rooftops makes me all nostalgic. Stars are our only witness. With no clouds in the sky, the temperature has dropped rapidly and I keep having to pull on my shifter strength for warmth. I miss my leather catsuit, it's so much warmer than the awful rags I'm wearing.

In front of me, Lennox is almost as quiet as I am, but his heavier weight occasionally makes the shingles crackle. It shouldn't be audible for any humans though, unless they're sleeping in the attic.

Because the guys got a tour of the estate, Lennox has taken the lead. Women and men sleep in separate buildings, which would explain why there are so few children. If the entire cult only has one new child each year, they'll go extinct soon. It's not surprising that they took us in without any hesitation. They need new blood.

We stop on top of one of two identical buildings that are facing each other. The women's house. If we were to stay here, this is where I'd end up. Not that I have any intentions of staying in this cult. It's a bit too tree-y for me.

Lennox lets me climb to the edge of the roof first. We're in luck, one of the windows on the first floor is open. I can't hear any breathing noises or movement from right under us, so it's probably a storeroom or bathroom. Using a drainpipe to hold on to, I climb down and vault through the window. The hinges are well-oiled and it doesn't make a sound. I land on all fours, my senses on high alert as I take in the dark room.

The floor and walls are covered in turquoise tiles, many of them cracked with age. Showers without curtains or screens are to my right while three basins are on the left. A bathroom. The floor is still wet, so I adjust my gait slightly to avoid any squelching sounds.

Lennox arrives with an elegant roll, although that means that he's now all wet. Idiot.

"Not exactly luxury," he whispers. "So they all shower in front of each other?"

"Stop thinking with your dick. Let's find the Mother."

In the hallway, I let Lennox take the lead again since he's seems to have a thing for smelling female hormones. It makes sense from an evolutionary point of view, but I'm not sure I like it. I'd prefer if I could smell them just as well as him.

I follow him in silence while I listen to our surroundings. Everyone on this floor is asleep. Several of the women snore loud enough that even human observers would be able to hear them.

We stop in front of the very last door. Lennox nods in response to my unspoken question. This is where the Mother lives. The breathing inside is slow and regular. She's sleeping like all the others. Let's hope she's not a light sleeper.

I carefully push down the door handle, but the door won't open. I add a bit more strength just in case it's stuck, but no, it must be locked. In any normal situation, I'd assume that the woman inside the bedroom locked the door, but right now, I wonder if someone locked her in. It wouldn't surprise me.

I could pick the lock, but I don't have a key to lock it again, which means someone would realise in the morning. I don't want them to become suspicious just yet. Guess that's the end of the road.

Breathing in deep, I memorise her scent. Not that it'll be hard to spot a pregnant woman, but just in case.

"Shall we look for the father?" Lennox whispers. "Or shall we go to bed? If the other two are still sneaking around, we'd have some alone time." He snakes an arm around my waist and pulls me close. "We've not had that in a while."

"Not here," I hiss and step away from him, but he's right. Maybe we should use this opportunity. Once we're back home, it'll be hard to find time for just him and me. That's the problem with being in a relationship with three males at once. There's never enough time to give them all the same attention. It was hard enough before we had children and has only become worse since. Four hyperactive, crazy, mischievous children who love randomly running into our bedroom in the middle of night aren't exactly conducive to a physical relationship with my men.

A warm shiver runs down my back and ignites sparks of desire deep within my belly. Tomorrow's another day. We don't need to solve the murder tonight.

I smile at Lennox. "Let's head back."

As soon as the door of my bedroom closes behind us, his hands are on me, ripping the rags off my body. I laugh at his impatience and lift my arms to make it easier for him. The sweet scent of his arousal is turning me on. He wants me. His eyes glow with desire as his gaze rakes over my body.

"Kat," he whispers, and then his lips crash onto mine. We kiss, passion burning hot in both of us, turning it into a dance of lips, tongues, breaths. His fingers run down my back, his nails sharp like claws. I moan at the pain and before I know what I'm doing, I've got my teeth clamped on his shoulder, biting down hard.

Lennox groans and puts his hands on my head, holding me in place. He loves when I bite him.

"Let go," he mutters. "Give into it."

I know what he means. He wants us to be feral. Give into the animal within. My cat purrs at the suggestion. She likes being in control.

"I love it when you purr like that," he says huskily and I realise I've actually started purring aloud.

Alright then. Time to let go. As soon as I've made my decision, I notice how my posture changes slightly. I'm poised to pounce on my prey. And there he is, right in front of me. Ready to be taken.

I push him backwards, letting us both tumble to the floor, then rip down his trousers, loose as they are, exposing his hard cock. My prey. My mouth waters as I stare down at him. Mine.

I press a small kiss to the tip of his cock - my cock - before taking him into my mouth. Lennox gasps when I suck hard.

"Turn around," he instructs and guides me until my knees are on either side of him, my pussy above his head. I'm dripping and if he waited a bit longer, he could drink from me without having to even lift his head. He grabs my hips and makes me lower myself. When his tongue touches my sensitive clit, I almost bite off his cock.

He drives me crazy, his tongue doing clever things to my pussy, and I give back as good as I get, licking him, sucking him, massaging his balls the way he likes it. But it's not enough. And I don't have the patience to wait.

Lennox groans in protest when I turn around, but then groans in delight when I position his cock at my entrance. I push down on him until he's fully embedded within me. A sigh escapes me. Yes, that's exactly what I needed.

He grabs my hips, his nails biting deliciously into my skin, and tries to control my movements, but I hiss at him, and he lets go. It's my turn to be in control. I want to be the one who brings us to the edge.

I ride him, our rhythm growing faster and faster, and by the time I climax around him, I've forgotten all about trees and cults and murders.

Chapter Five

Morning comes at least four hours too early. I can't remember how I ended up in my own room, but I'm glad I'm there now. Angie stands by my bedside, scowling down at me. She's clearly not impressed that I'm still asleep.

If only she knew what I did last night. Since men and women sleep in separate buildings, I doubt they get a lot of chances to tumble in the sheets. Maybe it would help the general mood if they let people have sex from time to time. They could even have their trees watching, if that turns them on.

"Time to get up," Angie says sternly. "There's a lot of work to do. I've been told you'll be helping to decorate the Mother today. Usually, newbies are put on the cleaning roster, but we need everyone for the celebration preparations."

She puts some gloves on a chair, bright red like her robe. "Wear these. We don't touch the Mother with our bare hands. You missed breakfast, so you'll have to last until lunch."

What a great start to the day. I suck at being a cultist.

A handful of women are already in the courtyard, sorting through large wooden crates. Ladders have been erected that reach all the way to the top of the Mother. I don't recognise any of the women. Angie said she had to help in the kitchen and it makes sense that pregnant Mary wouldn't do physical work like this.

"Hi, I'm Kate," I introduce myself to the closest woman, a redhead in her forties. Her ruby robe clashes catastrophically with her ginger hair.

"Welcome to the Womb," she says with a smile. "I'm the Star."

"*The* Star?" I repeat.

"I will take the role of the Star in the ceremony tonight. Until the day after tomorrow, my given name doesn't matter."

"Is there anyone else involved besides the Mother, Father and you?"

"Of course." She looks at me as if I'm the most ignorant person she's ever come across. These cultists could really do with some respect for those not part of their group. "The Servant is yet to play her role while the Messenger has already completed his. And then there's the Child, of course, to be born from the Mother's womb."

"Does everyone play the same roles every year?" I ask her.

She looks at me as if I said something deeply offensive. "We don't *play*. We are chosen to symbolise our namesakes. This isn't acting. We're touched by the divine and our every move is controlled by them. Tonight, I will drink the mother's Gift so that She may guide me."

I flick a look at the growth at the trunk of the Mother tree. The tubes have been removed, but dark spots on the bark tell of where the cultists have taken sap from the tree in the past. I have to get my paws on some of that sap, the Gift. I assume it has some sort of hallucinogenic properties. Maybe something to make the cultists easier to control. I'll find out. If I get a sample, I can get one of the cats to bring it back to Lily and M.E.O.W. We're surrounded by Ryker's cats. They watch from the rooftops and wait in the shadows. I can hear and smell them, although the humans are oblivious to the sudden influx of felines. A few of the scents are familiar. Cats that we've had previous dealings with will be the best messengers since they won't complain when we put a string or collar around their necks to carry a scribbled note.

"Help us open these crates," the Star says. "We will go on the ladders and you can lift up what we require."

We work in silence, first removing nails from crates to open their lids, then taking out the decorations stored within and spreading them out on the ground, sorting them by kind and colour. The golden glass baubles are my favourites, each of them clearly handmade. They aren't perfect, some have impurities in the glass, others aren't quite round, but that's what I like about them.

Once everything is sorted, the other women climb the ladders and call for the ornaments they want me to pass up. I have the most demanding job, but I don't mind. It's exercise to keep me in shape. Although I do have to resist the urge to stretch like a cat from time to time.

The women seem content not to talk, but I need information. It's why I'm here. Decorating a massive tree isn't important. Finding Geoffrey Baker's killer is. Not because I really care about him. I don't. But I don't want to go back to being bored. Until the end of our holiday, this is the perfect mission to keep busy.

"Is there some special meaning to the ornaments?" I ask the oldest woman while passing her a silver star.

"There is, but it would take too long to explain it all," she says not unkindly. "You arrived at both a grand and a bad time. It will be great for you to witness the most important celebration of the year, but there's no time to teach you our ways like we usually would. Your training will have to come later. For now, trust that we know what we're doing and observe."

In silence. She doesn't say it, but her pursed lips make it very clear.

"I just want to make sure I don't make any mistakes," I say in a shaky voice. "I don't want to make a bad impression on my first day."

Her expressions softens. "That's alright, child. I remember how exciting yet scary everything was when I joined the family. It'll take time for you to learn our ways. Has anyone told you yet what will happen tonight?"

I shake my head.

"Pass me a red bauble. One of the small ones. Tonight, on the Eve of the Birth, the Mother and the Father will be reunited for the first time since the Conception eight months ago. The Father will give the Mother the Gift and will care for her during the many hours of labour. The Star and the Servant will stay with them to help in any way they can. In the meantime, the rest of us gather here in the courtyard to celebrate the great sacrifice the Creators made for us all. We will worship them until the Star arrives with the good news."

"That the Child has been born."

She smiles approvingly. "Yes. The Servant will then look after the Child until it's old enough to join the nursery. That's when the entire community become its parents."

"And what about the Mother and the Father? Will they not spend time with the Child?"

"Hand me two of the little stars. No, they will not. The Mother will continue to donate milk to the Child, but she won't feed it herself. It's not like she's the Child's mum. She was just a vessel for the Mother."

This is getting confusing. I wish they gave the human Mother and Father different names from the trees. But I suppose that's the point.

I couldn't imagine getting separated from my children after giving birth to them. It might be different for the cultists, though. They know from the start that they're not having a child as a couple, but that they're producing it for the entire cult.

Everything about it is planned and ritualised. Nothing is left to nature.

"I need another golden bauble."

I hurry to fulfil the older woman's wishes, playing my own role as best as I can. Meek, weak, desperate to be part of the Womb of the Tree.

"What about the Messenger?" I ask after a few minutes of silence. "The Star mentioned him."

"He has already done his job," she says, her focus on the golden-painted cone in her hands.

"What did he do? What was his task?"

A loud bell interrupts us. The woman looks almost grateful at the interruption.

"Lunch," she says cheerfully. "It'll only be some bread and cheese since they'll be busy cooking the feast for tonight. It's a pity that..."

She breaks off and climbs down the ladder without another word. I bet she was about to mention Geoffrey Baker, the cook. Maybe I can get her to talk more after lunch.

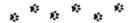

Despite the crowd, Lennox somehow manages to end up in the queue right behind me.

"Found anything?" he whispers, so quiet only I can hear. Everyone else in the hall is silent, so we're relying on our enhanced shifter senses to communicate. Humans will see our lips moving, but they won't be able to hear what we're saying.

"Got a lesson in their theology, but nothing connected to the murder. Yet. I feel like I'm getting closer."

"Same." He groans. "I've not worked this hard in... ever? Why did we think it was a good idea to pretend to be farmhands?"

"Because that's what they needed. Stop complaining. I had to alternate between crouching on the ground and reaching up a ladder. I really want to shift."

"I'd like to see their reaction to that. They'll either worship you or kill you."

"After what we saw yesterday, I'd guess the latter. Have they mentioned the Messenger to you?"

"No. But we got a fun story about how they choose the Father." He chuckles. "They have to make sure that he's fertile... Which is why there are usually two children each year, the holy one and one that's the result of male potency tests."

"Mary. She must be the one the potential Father candidate slept with."

"That's what we think, too, although we didn't get official confirmation. One of the men hinted that the guys and I might have to go through testing soon. They're running out of males who haven't been Fathers before. If necessary, they can repeat their role a second time, but to keep the gene pool sustainable, they try to have a new Father and Mother each year."

"You're *not* going to sleep with a cultist," I hiss. "I forbid it."

"Don't worry, you're the only cat in my life. You're the one who's greedy."

We've finally reached the buffet and fill our plates with thick slices of crusty bread and a variety of cheese. The only drink on offer is water. Let's hope they didn't infuse it with tree sap.

I once again sit with Angie and two of the women I just worked with, while the guys are at a table on the other side of the room. I force myself not to look in their direction. After all, they're just my brothers, adoptive brothers at that.

When the cacophony of chewing, cutlery hitting crockery (and the occasional tooth) and random swallowing sounds finally does down, Nikolaus gets up.

"I've been told we're on schedule with almost all preparations," he says in a booming voice that fills the room. "Well done, my family. If we all continue working together like this, we're going to have the best Birth Celebrations we've ever had."

He raises his glass and the cultists toast him with theirs. A water toast, how quaint.

Footsteps outside alert me just before the door is pushed open. A young woman hurries inside and heads straight to Nikolaus. She whispers to him. I focus my senses on them, but several people around me start chewing again and I can't hear what she's saying.

After a moment, he straightens again and clears his throat.

"I hear the Mother is starting to show signs of going into labour already, even though the Father hasn't given her the Gift yet. Star, Servant, you're both excused from your other duties and are to join her immediately. I will prepare the Gift so that the Father can give it to her as soon as possible."

Cheers break out and genuine joy reflects on the faces of the cultists. Even so, none of them start talking to voice their excitement.

"Everyone, please return to your tasks. I'm sure you all ache to complete them as fast as possible so we can start our celebrations. But don't forget: the Creators are watching us. Make them proud by completing your chores to the best of your ability. We wouldn't want to disappoint them, would we?"

That seems to be the signal for the believers to break into a whispered mantra. Their voices turn into a deep hum that reminds me of a beehive.

"Oh Mother tree, oh Father tree, we'll always serve and worship thee."

I move my lips to give the semblance of joining them, but inside, I'm cackling with laughter. I look at Nikolaus again and find his gaze is fixed on me. Knowing that I should pretend to be meek, I lock eyes with him. I can't help it. His lips quiver into a smirk and a shudder runs down my back. Something's wrong.

Chapter Six

I t only takes another hour to finish decorating the Mother tree. I have to say that I feel a strange pride when I look at our handiwork. Not that I placed any of the baubles and stars myself, but hey, I helped.

"Let's look at what the men did," one of the younger women suggests. "I wonder if they got the colour scheme confused again."

Ah, healthy competition. I like it.

"No time," another admonishes her. "You heard what Nikolaus said. Things are different this year. We have to be quick."

"What else is there to do now that we've decorated the tree?" I ask them.

They gasp in various stages of outrage.

"The *Mother*," the older woman who I helped earlier corrects. "It's important to use the correct language. It's an important part of worship."

I bow my head in fake deference. "I'm sorry."

"I understand that you're new and you have a lot to learn. Maybe stay quiet today. We wouldn't want you to offend the Creators on the most significant days of the year."

The guys would laugh if they could hear this. She asked me to shut up. Good luck with that. They've been trying it for years.

"I'm sorry," I say again, giving my voice a little quiver. I flutter my eyelashes, hoping to make it look like I'm about to cry.

The woman pats my shoulder, clearly buying my performance. "It's alright. Now you know. Follow me, let's see if we can help setting up the dining hall for later."

For the next two hours, I wipe tables and clean dishes. It's still just us women, with no men anywhere in sight. I'm surprised they let the guys and me stay in the same building, but they must have believed the brother story. Or maybe their strict gender separation doesn't apply to newbies. Either way, I'm glad when one of the women in charge finally tells us that we're done.

"Time to get dressed for the celebration," she says, clearly as excited as everyone else although she's trying her hardest to hide it. "Make sure your robes are clean and freshly ironed. You want to look your best tonight."

The women scurry off, but since I'm wearing my one and only robe, I have nothing to do.

"Excuse me," I ask a passing cultist. "Could you tell me where I can find Mary?"

"She's usually in the sewing room," she says and hurries off before I can find out more.

I didn't even know there was a sewing room, but it sounds like something even someone as pregnant as Mary could still do. The only time I ever use a needle is to sew up wounds, so this isn't exactly familiar territory. A young man outside the dining hall gives me proper directions. The sewing room turns out to be a large basement with several sewing machines and other gadgets I can't identify arranged on long tables. There's enough space for at least ten people, but the only one here is Mary. She's bent over a sewing machine, but it looks like she's using it as a pillow rather than working. Poor little thing. She must be really tired to fall asleep in this kind of place. I doubt Nikolaus looks kindly upon those who skive off work.

I slide onto the bench next to her. That movement wakes her and she sits up straight, looking at me in horror.

"I won't tell anyone," I promise quickly. "Don't worry."

She doesn't believe me. I don't blame her. Somehow, I don't think cultists would let her get off with falling asleep on an important occasion like today.

"How about we make a deal?" I try. "You answer some of my questions and in return, nobody will ever know that you nodded off."

Mary seems more comfortable with that. She nods, her eyes still wide and full of fear. I wonder what punishment she'd get. Surely nothing too bad, not in her condition?

She checks her watch. "We don't have much time. The celebrations will begin soon."

"Glad I woke you in time. Alright, let's start with the elephant in the room. Who's the father?"

Her lips begin to shake. I want her to pull herself together, but I'm worried that if I tell her to get a grip, it'll only make it worse. I remember being in thrall to pregnancy hormones. It was awful.

When she doesn't say anything, I make an educated guess. "Was it Geoffrey Baker?"

Fear gives way to confusion as she shakes her head. "No. Why would you think that? Is that what the others are saying? Is that the rumour?"

"No, just a wrong guess. So, if not him, then who was it?"

"I'm not supposed to know. It's supposed to be a secret."

"Wait, that doesn't make any sense. You'll have slept with whoever fathered your child. It's hard to do that without knowing who you're in bed with."

"You don't know our ways. You have so much to learn."

I sigh. "Enlighten me."

"I was Mother two years ago. They know I'm fertile. He chooses the men who have potential to be future Fathers. I'm not supposed to know, they blindfolded me, but I recognised his smell. Both their scents."

"Both?"

She looks down on the sewing machine, her entire body shaking. "I can't. No one must know."

"Did they... force you?"

"No! Of course not. I'm honoured to help choose the next Father. But... it wasn't just Luke. He's my baby's father. It was also..."

71

"Nikolaus."

Mary nods. "Everyone knows he can't father children, but he tried anyway."

I want to cut that man's throat. He took advantage of this young woman. Exploited his role as the leader of the cult. He should be taking care of his family, not his own needs.

The pain in her eyes is striking. She's suffered. And since she was born into this cult, she's probably suffered all her life.

"Thanks for telling me," I say softly. "Next question. How did Geoffrey die?"

"You will understand once you're initiated. It's all part of our ways."

"Murder is part of your ways?"

She looks up, confusion glinting in her pretty eyes. "He wasn't murdered. He-"

A loud bell rings, cutting her off. I want to cover my ears. My sensitive hearing doesn't do well with bells. It also makes me want to roll around the floor and chase after the sound. Stop it, kitty. No time for fun and games.

Mary gets up with a groan, supporting her bump with her hands. "We have to go. It's about to begin."

I follow her as she waddles towards the courtyard. "How did he die?"

She just shakes her head. When we round a corner, others join us and it becomes impossible to ask Mary any more questions. I lost my chance. Oh well. I suppose it's time to have a party and see what this celebration is all about.

Darkness is falling quickly. It's cold and I wish my robe was made from a thicker fabric. It smells like snow is imminent. The cultists around me don't seem to mind the cold. They're the happiest I've seen them so far.

Once again, men and women stand in separate groups, chatting animatedly with each other. For once, they behave like normal human beings. As normal as humans can be.

I lose Mary in the crowd, which is astonishing considering the size of her. I bet she's done it on purpose. She doesn't want to give me another chance to prod her with questions. For now, I'm fine with waiting. The excitement humming in the air is infectious. A small stage has been erected to the right of the Mother tree, but for now, it's empty.

"Kate!"

Gryphon waves from the other end of the courtyard where he and my other two mates are standing with two huge, bearded men. They appear to be brothers, maybe even twins.

I weave my way through the crowd until I reach them. The men give me a disapproving look, but then move on, leaving me alone with my mates.

"Found anything?" I whisper.

"Yes," Gryphon smiles triumphantly, "we got to meet the Father. The man, not the tree. He's a bit of an idiot. Maybe it's good that the child won't be raised by him."

"Where is he now?"

"With the Mother, the Star and the Servant," Ryker recites, a proud grin curving his lips. "I'm starting to get the hang of this. I can almost see the capital letters in my mind when I hear them talk. Anyway, I don't think the Father is of any importance. His scent wasn't familiar, I doubt he was at the clearing where the cook was killed. And as Gryphon says, he's not the brightest bulb in the chandelier."

"What about you?" Lennox asks. "You smell of hormones."

"Yes, I had a little chat with Mary, the pregnant woman who isn't the Mother. What she said made me want to kill Nikolaus, but I'm being sensible."

I fill them in on what I learned, as little as it is.

"Bastard," Ryker exclaims. "Even if he didn't murder Geoffrey, we should make sure he doesn't stay in control of this cult. It's not good for anyone, especially not the females."

I nod. "I completely agree. Let's wait until after the festivities, though. I have a feeling we might learn something by observing their celebrations."

"Do you think there'll be wine?" Gryphon asks, licking his lips. "I don't want to have to drink water again. It's not a party without lots of wine."

"You're a spoilt siren, you know that, right?" I tease him. "The rest of us didn't grow up with parties, let alone wine."

He shrugs. "Can't help that I'm posh. Not that I look it in these robes."

Another bell chimes and silence falls over the courtyard like a thick blanket. I turn around just in time to see Nikolaus staring at me from the little stage. His gaze lingers on me for another second before sweeping across the crowed. He smiles as he looks down on his disciples.

"We have reached the Eve of the Birth," he begins, his voice strong and full of fake warmth. "The Mother has drunk the Gift and is set to give birth soon, maybe even before midnight. It's sooner than expected, but if it's the will of the Creators, then so

75

be it." He looks up at the Mother tree to his right while making a dramatic pause. "We are truly blessed, my family, to be celebrating together. We want for nothing. We have everything we need and more. Most importantly, we're closer to the Mother and the Father than ever before. Tonight, they will illuminate us with their wisdom and love. They will rejuvenate our souls as we celebrate our Creators. We are the Chosen ones, my friends, my family. We can rejoice in the knowledge that we are safe from evil while we follow the righteous path."

The cultists cheer and clap. They lick up his words, desperate for more.

I wonder what their ideology says about people who aren't on the *righteous path*. Do we all die in some apocalyptic event? Will we be pulled down into the earth by tree roots? Killed by falling branches?

"While we wait for the Birth, we shall eat, drink and be merry. But first, let's listen to the song Carol has prepared for us."

One of the women who worked on decorating the tree with me joins Nikolaus on the stage. That must be Carol. She closes her eyes, takes a deep breath, and starts yowling like a cat in heat. I need every ounce of self-control to stop myself from laughing. She's awful. Not a single note is what it's supposed to be. Why would she volunteer to sing when she clearly can't sing?

I look at the cultists around me. Most look pained, tortured or embarrassed. Nikolaus is the only one who seems to enjoy Carol's singing. I wish I had ear plugs. This is awful.

"Make it stop," Ryker whispers. "Please make it stop."

Poor him. His hearing is the most sensitive of us all.

By the time Carol finally finishes her howling, I'm ready to leap onto the stage to strangle her. She gives us a short bow, then re-joins the crowd. I really hope someone will tell her not to ever do this again. Even I would have been better and I can't sing in the slightest.

"How lovely," Nikolaus cheers and I think he's serious. Wow, his hearing must be impaired. "Thank you, Carol, that was wonderful. Now, I'm sure you're all eager to hear who this year's Match will be."

I exchange a look with my mates. They're just as clueless as I am. Match? Yet another role? Nobody's mentioned that before.

Nikolaus dramatically clears his throat. "I'm so pleased to announce that our match is Tricia!"

Applause echoes through the courtyard as a middle-aged woman makes her way through the crowd. She leans on a walking stick that's been wrapped in golden tinsel, the same material some of the ornaments are covered in. I've only seen her from a distance before. She's beaming, her eyes sparking with pure joy and pride. As soon as she's on the stage, Nikolaus hands her a cable with a little plastic box on the end.

"Tricia, you've been a light to us all this year, which is why you've been chosen as our Match. On my signal, you may press the button."

He makes a long pause, keeping us all in suspense. Tricia looks a little unsure, but she waits for his signal. Finally, he smiles and nods at her. "Give us the light of the Mother."

She flicks a switch on the box and the lights in the Mother tree are turned on, sparkling like a hundred stars in the darkness. The lights had already been installed when I'd started helping with decorating the tree, so I had no part in their placement, but I have to say that I feel a little proud of how amazing the Mother looks like. The tiny lamps reflect in the shiny ornaments, enhancing the sparkle.

"Beautiful," one woman next to me sighs, and I tend to agree. Looking at this brightly lit tree gives me a strange warm feeling in my belly. I don't know why. Maybe because it's cold and dark, and the lights are the complete opposite. I doubt it's because of some deities living in the trees.

"Well done," Nikolaus says and helps Tricia off the stage. "Now, let's eat and drink while we wait for the Birth."

Chapter Seven

The courtyard bursts into activity. Tables are brought into the centre, bowls and plates piled onto them. Giant steaming pots are set up on either end. Is that wine I smell? Warm wine? Gryphon will see that as an abomination. I, on the other hand, am curious. It smells delicious. Spicy, sweet, and, best of all, hot. I keep having to draw on my shifter energy to keep warm.

An orderly queue forms along the tables and we join it, waiting our turn to be given a bowl of soup, some bread and a mug of steaming wine. I want to return to our previous place, but someone touches my elbow. I whirl around, almost spilling my wine, but it's just Angie.

"Join us over here," she says in a voice that is more an order than an invitation. She probably disapproves that I was talking to men all by myself. My poor little virtue, I hope she's still intact. I bite back a grin and follow her to a group of women. Most of them were part of the decoration crew, but there's also Mary, Carol, and some others I've not met yet. The pregnant girl has been given a chair to sit on while the rest of us stand.

"Isn't she beautiful?" Angie sighs. It takes me a moment to realise she's talking about the tree.

The other women make sounds of agreement while I sip on the wine, too curious to wait any longer. I swirl the warm liquid around my tongue, trying to separate all the different aromas. Cinnamon, clove, lemon zest, star anise, sugar. And something else, a faint umami taste that I'm not sure humans would even detect. I can't identify it and that frustrates me to no end. I take another sip, and another, until my mug is empty, yet I've still not solved the mystery.

"Thirsty?" Angie looks at me disapprovingly, but I don't care. A pleasant warmth is spreading inside me. Now I could do with a fireplace, a blanket and three naked mates. Sadly, I won't get any of those things, at least not now.

"It's very nice, what's in it?" I ask her.

"It's a secret recipe. We call it mulled wine."

"What does *mulled* mean? Like in mulling over something? Will this wine make us think?"

Mary chuckles but quickly catches herself, forcing away her smile. Poor girl. I wonder if she's ever been away from the cult. I doubt it.

"We're only allowed one mug each, so you'll have to stick to tea or water from now on," Angie says sternly before turning to Carol. "Lovely singing, dear. So full of emotion."

I stare into my empty mug, trying very hard not to laugh. While the women talk in hushed voices, I only half-listen while observing the crowd. As always, men and women have segregated into separate groups, although that rule doesn't seem to apply to Nikolaus. He's standing in the centre of a gaggle of young women who all look at him with awe and adoration. It makes me want to throw up my wine. They seem to think he's better than them and it's clear that he likes it that way. I wonder if he's taken advantage of more girls than just Mary. It's likely. He's the kind of person to take what he wants because he thinks it's his divine right. He even invented a religion to have power over others.

It reminds me why we're here. To solve a murder, not to ogle over brightly lit trees.

"Why are we celebrating in this courtyard?" I ask when silence falls in our little group. "The Father was also decorated, wasn't he?"

Angie seems to approve of that question and gives me a genuine smile. "Today, we celebrate the Birth,

83

which is the domain of the Mother. The Father gets decorated in the same way because we want to honour both of them equally. In four months' time, during the Sowing of the Seed ceremony, we'll be celebrating in the other courtyard, again with both of them fully decorated."

Sowing of the Seed. Oh my. I want to laugh hysterically at that. Do they have sex in public to create the next holy baby? I wouldn't put it past them. Nikolaus probably presides over it all, watching, perving, getting off on it.

When everyone's finished their soup, we move onto the main course, a thick slice of turkey meat along with various sides that we can help ourselves to. I wouldn't have combined most of those things if I'd had to come up with the meal - why would I want both sprouts and cabbage, aren't they kind of the same thing? - but I have to admit that everything is rather tasty. I just wish I could get a second mug full of wine, but Angie is keeping a hawkish eye on me, making sure I stick to the rules. Maybe I should remind her that I'm not even a full member of the cult yet. Nor will I ever be. One tree worshipping ceremony is enough for me.

After dinner, some teenagers collect our dirty dishes, while the men fold away the tables. Nikolaus appears on the stage again, holding a mug of steaming wine. Rub it in. I bet he's allowed as much as he wants.

"My dear family, children of the Womb," he begins, smiling down on us like a proud father. "It is time now for me to read you the story, the most important story of your lives. I-"

A bell rings in the distance. Gasps follow it like an echo. Something important is happening.

"The Star!" Nikolaus exclaims. "The Star is coming!"

That means the baby has been born. Next to me, two women hug while another starts to cry tears of joy. At least that's what I hope they are.

"Star of the Night," Nikolaus proclaims solemnly. "Come to those of us who watch. Come to those of us who listen. Come to those of us who know."

The cultists repeat his words in a whisper, like a prayer.

"Star of the Night. Join us in our midst and tell us the good news."

The Star, the red-haired woman from earlier, steps into the courtyard. She's changed into a white gown not unlike my own robes and carries a large scroll. Before ascending to the stage, she curtsies to the tree.

"I am the Star of the Night," she says in an ethereal voice very different from how she spoke at our previous encounter. "And I proclaim that the Child has been born. Sown by the Father, carried by the Mother, blessed by the world."

She unrolls the scroll in one dramatic movement. "And it shall be known that that the Child is of male sex and healthy from top to root. Its name has been given to him by the Mother and the Father and it shall be Rowan. Rejoice, Children of the Womb, for your family has grown."

Rowan. That's actually kind of cute. Certainly better than Fir or Pine.

Nikolaus bows his head to her. "Thank you, Star, for this wonderful message. You may return to the Child while we celebrate its arrival."

More celebrating. Goody good. I search out my mates in the crowd and find all three of them looking at me. How adorable.

Now that the baby's arrival has been announced, the mood is less formal. The men get to refill their mugs with wine while us women are only allowed some peppermint tea. Disgusting.

I aimlessly walk around, slowly moving towards my mates without making it too obvious that they're my destination. While weaving through the crowd, I listen to their conversations, hoping to hear Geoffrey mentioned. It's a long shot but that's what we're here for, after all.

Sadly, I have no luck today. Most of the cultists talk about how excited they are about the new baby, how they like the name, how they enjoyed the food. Boring. At one point, I think I hear my own name and turn just in time to see Nikolaus bent over Mary, whispering to her. I start heading back in that direction, but someone bumps into me from behind, spilling hot tea all over my back.

"I'm so sorry," a deep voice says. A man I've not met yet. "I didn't see you there."

Sure you didn't. Idiot.

"Are you alright?" he asks. He's a young man, early twenties at most, with eyes as cold as the night.

"No thanks to you," I shoot back before realising I'm meek Kate and not moody Kat. "Sorry. It surprised me. I better get changed."

All I have is my rags to change into. Maybe I can get another robe from someone.

On the way out of the courtyard, I look over where Nikolaus was talking to Mary, but he's left, leaving her sitting alone on her chair. She looks upset for some reason.

"Kate, wait!"

Angie hurries after me, the cultists making way for her to let her through. They didn't do that for me earlier.

"You need to come with me," she says without meeting my eyes. "Nikolaus wants to see you."

Ominous. Is it normal for him to want to talk to the newbies in the middle of the big celebration or is something amiss? Did Mary tell him about the questions I asked her? Only one way to find out.

I follow her into a part of the compound I haven't been before. We pass other cultists on the way, but they barely spare us a glance. I extend my senses, trying to find my mates. There are some old traces from several hours ago, but nothing fresh. At least that means he's only summoned me, not all of us.

The girl leads me to the second floor of a narrow building. She takes two steps at once as she sprints up the stairs. I follow with an amused smile while also going through a hundred different scenarios that might be about to happen. I only have two small knives hidden in my boots as well as some poison darts tucked into a secret pocket. Since we're dealing with humans and are here to gather information rather than to assassinate them, I had to leave all my favourite blades at home.

I'd feel better with a knife in my hand, but I'm probably overthinking the situation.

We stop in front of an oak door which doesn't quite match the rest of the building. Angie knocks, then leaves without giving me another look.

Chapter Eight

"Come in," Nikolaus calls from the other side and I enter, tense and alert. He sits behind a desk very similar to the one I once had at the M.E.O.W. headquarters. Behind him, two full-length windows give a perfect view of the two courtyards and most of the cult's compound. So this is where he keeps check on his followers.

The two trees – sorry, the *Mother* and the *Father* – are even more imposing from up here, showing their massive size compared to the buildings around them. The decorations sparkle in the afternoon sun. The women will be pleased to know that the Mother looks better than the Father. We did a good job.

"Kate, thanks for coming," he says with a smile that doesn't reach his eyes. "I hope you're enjoying the celebrations. I hear you helped with decorating the Mother earlier."

Yes, and you probably watched me from here. But I don't say that, I just smile and listen.

"I wanted to take a moment and talk with you about why you chose to join us," he continues. "There are many shelters in Attenburgh that you could have gone to. Why us?"

"We were given a pamphlet," I say, repeating what we'd already told him yesterday. Why is he suddenly doubting us? He accepted it without question last night.

"There are many people handing out leaflets on the streets. Again, why us?"

I take a deep breath. "I don't know. Something felt right about it. When I read about the Womb of the Tree, I thought it sounded like a place that could become our home, not just a place to sleep. Was I wrong?"

I'd hoped he'd backtrack and tell me how much he wants us to be part of his family, but from the frown marring his face, he's not satisfied. I'm starting to think that he knows who we are. Should I pretend I had some vision of the holy trees? No, that would be too much. Too obvious.

"We rarely get strangers who come with their entire family," he says after a moment. "Lone men or women, yes, but not four of them at once. And not in the week of our most important celebration of the year. You understand why I'm wondering if this is too good to be true?"

I give him my most innocent smile. "Maybe it was meant to be. Maybe it was fate."

"There is no fate. All our destinies are directed by the Creators who know what's best for us. Either way, there have been some events recently that make it hard for me to trust. I hate that I'm feeling like this, but I have to think rationally. Especially when I hear that you've been asking questions. Too many questions. Therefore, I'd like you to prove that you're here with pure intentions."

Not good. "How can I prove it?"

He pushes the mug in front of him across the desk. I'd thought it contained tea or coffee, but now that I focus on it, the scent is nothing like what I expected. It's familiar, though. I smelled it all morning while decorating the tree.

"This contains a drop of the Gift, the holy essence given to us by the gracious Father. Whoever consumes it is compelled to tell the truth. The Father commands it."

A truth serum. Curious. I know several recipes to make one, but none of them involve tree sap. This little mission is proving most interesting. I'll have to

91

tell Bethany when we're back, maybe she can replicate it with normal tree sap. So far, I've learned that they use the Mother's sap to induce birth and I think the Star also mentioned she'd drink it to prepare for her role. Now Nikolaus says that the Father's sap has yet another purpose. Would the Mother's sap have the same effect? Maybe that's why the Star drank it, to ensure that she'd only tell the truth when announcing the baby's birth.

But the biggest question is, will the serum affect me, or does it only work on humans? Only one way to find out. If I realise that the truth is spilling from my lips, I'll simply cut the guy's throat.

"What about my brothers?" I ask, pretending to be scared. "Can they be here while I drink it?"

Nikolaus smiles at me, but there's no warmth in it. He seems to enjoy making me uncomfortable. "They're busy. You wouldn't want them to delay our festivities, would you?"

"No... Of course not."

"Good girl. Now drink. Don't worry, it tastes nice and sweet."

I take the mug, making sure to make my hands tremble a little. I want him to think that he's got me in a vulnerable position.

He couldn't be further from the truth.

I take a sip, surprised at how good it tastes. Honey and vanilla with a hint of cardamom. Delicious.

"Drink it all up," Nikolaus instructs and I'm happy to oblige. While the liquid warms my stomach, I am on high alert, monitoring my body and mind for any signs of change. I don't feel any different. Good.

"What's your name?" he asks, his eyes boring into me.

"Kate."

Yay. I can lie. That means I can give him a show. This might work out to my advantage after all.

"And where are you from?"

"I was born in Attenburgh, but my parents travelled a lot, taking me with them. When they died, I was passed from one orphanage to the next."

"How sad." Not that he sounds sympathetic at all. He couldn't care less about my sob story. "Why did you come here?"

"Because we were given a pamphlet and needed a home. We-"

Suddenly, my tongue grows heavy. It feels like it's becoming too big for my mouth. My lips are pushed open as my tongue expands. I gasp for breath. What the fuck is happening?

"I may have lied when I said that it makes you tell the truth," Nikolaus says, looking genuinely happy at seeing me struggle with my oversized tongue. "However, it does show when someone lies. And you lied, a lot. From the strength of your reaction, you didn't speak a single word of truth. You're not an orphan, your name isn't Kate and you're certainly not here to seek refuge. I knew it!"

The triumphant look painted across his face makes me want to puke. Not that I'd get anything out of my mouth just now. I can barely breathe through my nose, and it feels like my tongue is still growing. Seems I underestimated him.

Oh well. There's a solution to it. Time to kill.

Moving faster than his eyes can see, I pull a knife from my boot and point it at him. I'd love to say some clever things, but I can't speak, so the gesture will have to do.

"If you kill me, you won't get the antidote," he says calmly. "You'll die without it."

He's bluffing. Or is he?

Before I make a decision, there's one thing left to try. I turn away from him so he can't see my face, then pull on my shifter strength and direct it to my mouth. My bones crack as my jaw shifts. My skin itches like crazy when fur pushes to the surface, but I keep a firm control on the partial shift. I've had a lot of time to practise while babysitting four kittens. With them in the house, I couldn't always shift fully, so I've become an expert at only transforming some body parts. The kids find it hilarious when I do it. They don't have that kind of control yet and they won't for a long time, so they find it very impressive.

As soon as I shift back to fully human, my tongue is its normal size again. Thank the purring cat in the sky. Triumphantly, I turn around to Nikolaus and give him a wide grin to make sure he realises that I'm no longer affected by his potion.

"I won't need an antidote," I say sweetly. "And I think it's time we talk properly."

His eyes widen, but I respect how he doesn't freak out.

"How?" he asks in a surprisingly calm voice.

"Tricks of the trade. So, let's lay our cards on the table. You're right. I lied. And I'm not here to become part of your cult. I'm here to solve a murder."

"Murder?" he asks, confusing shining through his arrogant mask. "There hasn't been a murder."

That's definitely not the reaction I was expecting. Why does that confuse him?

"Geoffrey Baker," I say firmly. "Killed by a tree. Remember?"

"That wasn't murder." His voice is flat, devoid of all emotion. I'm having a hard time getting a read on him.

"So he swallowed the tree voluntarily and killed himself in the process?"

"You wouldn't understand. If you were an actual acolyte, you'd eventually get to learn about the sacred sacrifice Geoffrey made. As you're not, you will never know."

"A sacrifice? You sacrificed him to the trees?"

"As I said, you wouldn't understand."

I'm having a hard time controlling my anger. I hate being patronised. "You're right, I don't. But if you don't want the authorities to convict you for murder, you'll have to do better than that."

"That's who you work for? The police?"

I chuckle. "No. Most definitely not. Let's say I'm a freelancer."

"That makes things easier. I thought I'd have to talk to my contacts in the police. They have strict instructions not to interfere with our business."

He bribes them. How lovely. That would explain why Lily isn't leaving the case to the authorities.

After Lady Lara's death, the town council voted for a successor I certainly wouldn't have voted for. Weak, easy to manipulate and deep in the pockets of various people. Not that I care. I'm done with politics. Any interest I had in what went on in the town hall died with Lady Lara.

"So, a *sacred* sacrifice," I try again. "But I saw the blood in the guest house. You kept him there against his will."

"What makes you say that?"

"I know it was him who stayed in there. If he volunteered to be sacrificed, then why lock him in?"

Nikolaus sighs. "It's not like you're going to tell anyone. To turn into the Messenger, one has to undergo a transformation. It can be painful. It can make people want to change their minds. Geoffrey agreed to be locked into a room during the transformation phase so that he wouldn't hurt him or others. Once he became the Messenger, he was released."

"And killed."

"How else is he supposed to bring the message to the Creators? It is the purest way. By joining with a tree, he has a direct connection to the Mother and the Father." He runs a hand through his hair, suddenly looking a little emotional. "No one will ever be as close to them. I envy our Messengers, I truly do. One day, I hope to take on that role myself. But not until my family is in a situation where I can leave them."

He's crazy. Mad. Deluded. That shouldn't be news to me, but I thought he had the best grip on reality out of all of them. Cult leaders usually do.

"What now?" he asks.

"Now, you die."

Chapter Nine

"**I**'m not supposed to kill you," I say while swirling the blade in my hand. He watches me calmly, although his heartbeat betrays his growing fear. "But I rarely follow the rules. I see three ways this could end. One, I kill you and walk away, closing the case with a remark that the murderer is deceased. Your cult can continue doing what they do as long as they don't kill anyone else. And you'll have to swear to keep your dick in your robes."

"What are the other two ways this can end?" he asks, his voice perfectly relaxed. There might even be a trace of sarcasm there.

"Option two, I leave you alive and tell the authorities about what's been going on. But since you already mentioned that you have contacts within the police, that might not be very effective.

Finally, option three. I torture you until you tell me who else was involved in killing Geoffrey Baker. Then I end your life and hand the others over to the police." I stop playing with my knife and point it at him. "In two out of three, you die. Any last words?"

"Don't you want to be saved?"

Not what I expected him to say. "What?"

"This is your one and only chance to save your soul. Join us and devote your life to the Creators. We could use people like you."

"Are you trying to convert me?"

He gives me a wry smile. "That was always the plan."

"Sorry, not interested. I'm too sane to pray to trees. And that says a lot. I'm not sure many people would describe me as sane. Least of all my mates."

"Then I'm afraid we'll have to part ways at this point."

He still thinks he has the upper hand. Too confident for his own good, that's for sure. Deluded yet intelligent enough to compensate for it.

Footsteps down below alert me that we won't be alone for much longer. Someone's walking up the stairwell. I have thirty seconds, maybe less.

Old Kat would have simply cut his throat. But annoyingly, I've developed a conscience. Motherhood hasn't been good for my assassin lifestyle. I don't want to kill him like this. Not while he's defenceless. In a fight, yes, I'd extinguish his life without a second thought. But if I was to draw my knife along his throat now, it would be murder. I wouldn't be any better than him. Worse, actually, because at least he thinks he didn't kill Geoffrey. He just assisted in a sacrifice.

But then I think of Mary. I'd be doing her and other women a service. She could be free, if she wants to be.

"Time to decide," Nikolaus says softly. By now, even his human hearing must have picked out on the person huffing and puffing up the stairs.

He's still smiling. I want to cut it off his face with my blade. Maybe I should. As a starter. And then I can still cut his throat after.

Only a few more seconds. Mary's sad eyes flash into my mind. She needs to get out of here, away from him, and this is the way it can be done. I can't allow this to continue. The women. The yearly sacrificial murders. Who knows how long they've been doing this. If his body hadn't been found by accident, then they would have continued, year after year. This isn't just about Geoffrey Baker. I don't really care about him. But I know what it's like to grow up in an organisation that thinks you no more than a slave. I was given help to escape the Pack. Maybe it's time for me to return the favour.

"Do you have any regrets?" I ask him just when the person stops outside the door. Nikolaus just looks at me, not saying a word. I doubt he has. I doubt he has any remorse for what he's done. It's all part of his religious beliefs. Usually, I'd say live and let live, believe and let believe, but not if it ends in suffering for others.

The knock on the door is the sign to strike. I leap over the desk and before Nikolaus can even react, my blade is pressed hard against his throat. This isn't going to be an elegant kill. There will be blood on my white robe. The person outside is a witness. Not as sleek as I like to have my assassinations, but I'm out of options.

In the distance, Carol starts to sing again, just as bad as before. Maybe even worse. It's the perfect soundtrack for Nikolaus' demise.

I slowly run the knife along his throat, cutting deep, while holding my other hand over his mouth to avoid him from crying out. He gurgles, he struggles, he dies.

Another knock. The scent is slightly familiar, a male who I've met at the celebrations. Nobody important.

"Just a minute!" I shout as if I didn't just kill a man. It feels good. I realise I'm smiling. I missed this.

Wiping my blade on his red robes, I turn away from him. Nikolaus is dead. Now how to proceed? He can't become a martyr. That wouldn't help Mary nor all the others who'll be sacrificed in the future as so-called Messengers. No, I need to get them to see sense. Face reality.

"Wait downstairs," I tell the man.

"I need to talk to Nikolaus!" he shouts back.

"He's otherwise occupied. Sowing his seeds. Get it?" I fake a deep groan to add to the illusion.

Footsteps hurry away from the door and down the stairs. Good. He either believed that Nikolaus was having his fun with me or he's about to alert everyone else. Either way, I have some time. What I need is advice from my men. I don't want to make this decision alone.

I whistle as loud as I can, using a frequency only Ryker and Lennox will be able to hear. Hopefully, Gryphon is with them.

Gryphon. That gives me an idea. It's a bit unorthodox and he won't be happy about it, but it'll be the easiest way to deal with the situation. I'll just have to make it up to him.

By the time they arrive, Carol has stopped screeching. They burst into the room without knocking.

"Told you," Lennox grins as soon as he takes in the scene. "I win."

"We made a bet on whether you'd killed him or not," Gryphon explains. "Ryker's the only one who thought you wouldn't."

"Only because someone had to bet against you two," the cat in question complains. "It's not a game otherwise if everyone's on the same side."

He looks me up and down. "Are you alright?"

"Why wouldn't I be?"

"It's been a while since your last kill."

I shrug. "He deserved it. But now we have a leaderless cult to deal with."

Gryphon sighs. "That could quickly turn into a bad situation. A martyr is impossible to kill again."

"Exactly. Which is why I need you."

He cocks his head. "What for?"

"After Carol's singing, I'm sure the crowd would be grateful for someone with a real feel for music. Who better than a siren? You could weave something into your song, something to make them disband."

Gryphon doesn't look happy at all, just as I predicted. He hates using his siren powers on humans, especially when they're innocent.

"Is there no other way?" he asks. "Maybe we can reason with them. Tell them not to kill anyone ever again."

Ryker chuckles. "They're humans. It's what they do. No, Kat is right. Your magic is the cleanest solution."

Gryphon runs a hand through his hair and sighs. "I think encouraging them to disband right away might be too direct. It's too far from their natural desires and will cause conflict in their minds. I'd have to weave a really powerful song to persuade them and it might drive some of them crazy."

"What if you give them the impression that the order came from the trees?" I suggest. "A divine message? That way the thought doesn't just pop into their heads but is conveyed to them by the beings they worship."

"I've never tried to impersonate a tree."

Lennox laughs. "There's a first time for everything."

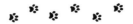

Gryphon starts his song before we even reach the courtyard. It'll make them ignore us as we make our

105

way to the stage. His music wraps itself around me in a warm, loving embrace. It tingles on my skin, causing a pleasant shiver to run down my back. I love it when he sings to me.

The effect is much stronger on the cultists. They sway from side to side in rhythm to the music, wide smiles on their faces, their eyes closed, their posture relaxed. They look a lot happier all of a sudden. Killing Nikolaus was the right choice. It gives them all a chance of a new life. Who knows how many of them weren't here voluntarily. They will be grateful in the future, even if it'll take them some time to get used to a life where not everything is controlled by scripture.

When we get to the stage, Gryphon changes the tune slightly. Since I'm not human, it doesn't work on me, but I can just about understand the intention of the song. Let it go. Start anew.

The longer he sings, the warmer I get. I look up at the brightly lit tree and smile. It's gorgeous in a completely non-religious way. I can appreciate the lights and the ornaments without believing that the tree is actually the creator of the world. Maybe we should make this a winter tradition. Put up a decorated tree to dispel the darkness and the cold.

By the time Gryphon sings his last note, the cultists have opened their eyes again and are all staring at the tree. They must believe that they've been spoken to by the Mother herself. They seem frozen, unblinking.

Gryphon takes my arm. "Time to go. We have about a minute before the magic wears off. Better to be gone by then."

"Will they remember us?"

"No. I've made sure of that. We better get rid of Nikolaus' body though. They'll think he's been called to the trees as a final act before disbanding the cult. Now they're free to go back into the world and live a good life."

"They'll still believe in their Mother and Father trees, right?" Ryker asks as we carefully make our way out of the courtyard, trying to avoid bumping into the unmoving cultists.

"Aye, they will. With time, that might fade. I'll assume they'll continue to come here to tend after the two trees, but who knows for how long that'll last. It might be interesting to observe them from afar. I rarely have the chance to see the long-term effects of my magic."

Nikolaus lies in a large puddle of blood. We don't have time to clean it up, so after Lennox and Ryker pick up the body, I move a rug on top of it. That should do. It's not like any crime scene investigators will come here. Nikolaus bribing the police to turn a blind eye will be to our advantage.

The guys carry him down the stairs.

"Where to now?" Ryker asks when we step back outside.

Something hits my face and I look up to see snowflakes dance down from the sky.

"Let's take him out of the compound and dump him in some corner for now. Lily can deal with the clean-up. We'll call her as soon as we get home."

Because that's where I want to be now. Home.

Epilogue

Maybe holidays aren't as bad as I thought.

After the excitement, craziness and death of the past days, it's quite nice to lie on the sofa, surrounded by my mates. I'm using Ryker's lap as a pillow while my feet rest on Gryphon's thighs. Lennox is in the kitchen making mulled wine. I can already smell the spices. No secret ingredients this time. I assume it was tree sap that gave it that extra flavour, but I'll likely never find out. I've made a mental note to check on Mary in the coming weeks, but that's the only involvement I'm planning to have with the ex-cultists.

I hope the baby will be taken care of by his parents. Lily said she'd make sure to keep track of what happens to the children. I've handed the case back to her. After all, she's the head of M.E.O.W., not me. Not anymore.

I'm quite content to lie here, having my feet massaged and my head scratched, while looking forward to drinking as much mulled wine as I want. They won't be able to stop me after just one mug. And if they try... this kitty has claws.

"It's still snowing," Gryphon mutters. "The kids might be stuck at Aunt Rose's for a while if this snowstorm continues. It'll take time to clear all the roads."

Ryker chuckles. "That wouldn't be a bad thing. It's quite nice to have some time alone, just for us grown-ups. Don't get me wrong, I love our kittens, but..."

I know what he means. If they were here, I wouldn't be stretched out on the sofa. And even if I somehow managed to, I'd have children sitting on top of me, begging me to play with them.

"I'll call them and tell them to stay a few more days," Gryphon says. "Aunt Rose will be fine with it. She adores them, no matter how much mess and work they create."

I nod, too sleepy to even talk. This is so cosy. Why did I think I didn't like holidays?

"The wine is done!" Lennox shouts from the kitchen.

I hope he doesn't expect us to get up. But no, he's being a lovely wolf and is already carrying a large tray into the living room. Good doggo. He'll get some head rubs for that later.

It's annoying to have to sit up to drink, but as soon as my hands are wrapped around my mug and the scent of spiced wine enters my nostrils, everything is fine again.

More than fine.

Lennox squeezes onto the sofa between me and Gryphon, then puts an arm around my shoulders. I snuggle against him while sipping my wine. Outside, the snow is falling, creating a natural barrier between us and the world. It's just the four of us now. No murders, no trees, no cults. And as much mulled wine as I want.

"I love you," I say, surprising myself.

The old Kat would have shuddered and pulled out her fur. But not me.

I'm okay with voicing my feelings. I'm okay with *having* feelings. Especially when they concern my handsome mates.

"Love you, too," Lennox whispers and kisses my cheek ever so gently.

"Obviously," Ryker says from my left and pats my thigh.

Gryphon doesn't say anything. He just smiles and starts to sing. The song wraps itself around me and I close my eyes, relaxing into the music.

Yup, holidays are good.

A purr breaks from my chest, an expression of love and contentment.

Purrrrr.

Happy Holidays! If this was your first encounter with the Catnip Assassins, start the series with Meow.

For more books, cats and shenanigans, subscribe to my newsletter: skyemackinnon.com/newsletter

Afterword

Dear readers,

I hope you enjoyed this crazy little festive story. I had no idea where it was going to go when I started writing and I was quite surprised myself when Kat stumbled upon a tree cult. Obviously, there's no Christmas in her world, but as usual she managed to bring her own twist to things. Kat is probably my most vocal character who never stops surprising me with her crazy behaviour and ideas.

I'm afraid to say that this really is the end of the Catnip Assassins. Kat has been part of my life for almost three years now and she's ready to retire. It was great fun revisiting her and her family, but she deserves to live the rest of her life without me (and you) observing her. Who knows, she might even end up turning into a law-abiding citizen with no assassinations at all. It's unlikely, but you never know.

As always, there are many people who were somehow involved in ensuring that this book gets written. Some might not even be aware of their role. A big thank you goes to my friends and co-authors Laura Greenwood and Arizona Tape, who gave Kat a wee shove when she stopped talking to me. Also thanks to Anika at Ravenborn Covers, without who this entire series might not even exist. And thanks to my assistant Tricia (did you spot yourself in the story?!), my beta readers, my street team, and my family.

Now, before I let you continue to the mulled wine recipe, my cat has a few words she'd like to say. She's been hovering next to the keyboard the entire time, so let's see what she wants to write.

jjjjjjjjjjjjjjjjjjjjjjjjjjjjjjjjjkkkkk kmmmmmmmmmmmmk

(*plus a whole lot of spaces that you can't see*)

Thanks, Sootie, for this very special message.

Lots of love,

Skye

PS If you want another festive story, take a look at *Below the Baubles*, a holiday special that's part of the Seven Wardens series (co-written with Laura Greenwood), a paranormal reverse harem full of Scottish mythology, although this holiday special involves a German Christmas market!

PPS Or if you're in the mood for aliens, I also have a very weird sci-fi romance called *Alien Abduction for Santa* in which Santa gets abducted by two female aliens... And they'll have great fun jingling his bells and inspecting his candy cane.

Mulled Wine Recipe

- 1 litre red wine (or grape juice)
- 50 ml rum (optional)
- 2 oranges, washed and cut into slices
- Juice from 2 oranges
- 1 star anis
- 7 cloves
- 2 cinnamon sticks
- 50g brown sugar

1. Add the wine, orange juice, orange slices and spices to a large pot. Heat slowly and let it simmer for an hour, but don't let it boil yet (that would get rid of the alcohol and we wouldn't want that).
2. Add rum and sugar and bring to the boil. Leave to steep for another half hour.

3. Pour through a sieve or strainer, reheat and enjoy.

About the Author

Skye MacKinnon is a USA Today & International Bestselling Author whose books are filled with strong heroines who don't have to choose.

She embraces her Scottishness with fantastical Scottish settings and a dash of mythology, no matter if she's writing about Celtic gods, cat shifters, aliens, or the streets of Edinburgh.

When she's not typing away at her favourite cafe, Skye loves dried mango, as much exotic tea as she can squeeze into her cupboards, and being covered in pet hair by her tiny demonic cat.

Subscribe to her newsletter:
skyemackinnon.com/newsletter

Printed in Great Britain
by Amazon

73176757R00073